'Remaking' the World:

MY BROTHER'S PANTS DON'T FIT ME

BY DR. IF

Illustrated by Constantin

COLOR EDITION

ISBN: 0615474861
ISBN-13: 9780615474861
Library of Congress Control Number: 2011927097

Website: KidsAndParentsPress.com

Publisher: KidsAndParentsPress.com,
509 St Andrews Blvd.
Lady Lake FL 32159

TABLE OF CONTENTS:

WHY DO I HAVE TO GROW WHERE I'M PLANTED?

Sometimes I wonder how a kid must feel
When Mom or Dad has died or gone away.
They often must arrange to eat a meal
Alone, or help at home instead of play.

If I remade the world, I'd make a rule
That every kid would have a backup squad.

A substitute would show up from a pool
Of volunteers: I know that's really odd!

In fact, adopted kids have found a home
With parents: not the ones they had when born.

They're part of families they call their own.
And wake up with a smiling face each morn.

A different fam'ly has rare gifts of love
Because of special challenges they face.

Each member puts the family above
The problem tasks that speed the daily pace.

So if a kid has love, no need to dream
Of something diff'rent from his present life.
Grow where you're planted! Join the team
That wants you to succeed despite all strife.

THE MESS IN MY ROOM!

I've often wondered why I have a Mom;
She's full of rules I daily must obey.
Without a Mom, I'd have few chores to do;
I'd always have the time to run and play.

My Mom expects that I will clean my room;
She likes it when I mow and trim the lawn.

I love recorded sound with its loud boom;
But Mom's the one who tells me "turn it DOWN!"

And then, there's so much homework to be done;
You'd think a kid could learn more from a game.

Those math and English tests: there should be none.
My goal is not the "Genius Hall of Fame!"

Yet in this world a Mom is good, I guess;
When I get hungry, food is always there.

Plus change of sheets and clothes for me to dress;
And helping me get well with her sweet care!

My Mom's the one who loves me when I'm good.
And when I'm bad and when I'm tired, too.
So I love Mom for more than just my food.
She's someone without which I cannot do!

BLAME THE UMP!

My Dad's a strict one when it comes to games;
He makes me work so hard to get it right.
I don't know why the ump he always blames,
But he won't let me start a home plate fight.

He stops me when he thinks I've told a lie,
And makes me do the things that Mommy said.

I wonder: to his Dad did he once try
To tell a fib? And then got sent to bed!

He says, "Now you must do your best in school;
Get 'A's' and 'B's' and try to be a champ."

To earn rewards, I'm using every tool
To please my Dad. Then I can go to camp!

I guess a Dad has got to be this way,
I've thought about it more than once, you see.

When I have kids some far off year and day.
I'll likely have one just the same as me.

So if at school a kid would say a word
That isn't nice about my loving Dad,
I'd raise my voice to prove that I was heard,
And say that he's the best I could have had!

SHE KISSED MY SORE SKINNED KNEE

My sister bugs me when I walk to school;
She's older and she acts like she's the boss.
I play games crossing streets but I'm no fool;
She doesn't like the tennis ball I toss.

I'm very sloppy when I make my bed;
My sister's always neat and lets me know:

She "rats me out", and that's the thing I dread,
My sis should not be dealing me a blow.

A sister doesn't understand a guy;
She fusses with her hair and can't play catch.

She's learning to make clothes and bake a pie.
And cookies? Guess I'll wait for her next batch!

In fact, my sister's not so bad at all;
It seems she's always looking out for me.

My Mom, she's not. But if I took a fall;
Sis would be there to kiss my sore skinned knee!

21

I hope that every guy who has a sis,
Will realize the benefits they have;
Not every bike you ride avoids a miss,
Sometimes it's good she's there to spread the salve!

MY BROTHER'S PANTS DON'T FIT ME!

I have two brothers, one of which is tall;
The pants he gives me when he grows a spurt.
Come past my shoe tops spilling over all,
Should he grow slower? Guess that wouldn't hurt!

My other brother gets the pants I toss;
He doesn't like to wear them when they're frayed.

The gain he gets from older brothers' loss,
Is very small; he seems a bit dismayed.

The competition brother-wise is strong.
We wrestle, pull and tug most every day.

But we forgive if anything goes wrong.
We have a lot of fun with games we play.

A brother is a friend who's always there.
No need to beg six buddies to go out.

For my whole life I'll know they both will care;
And buck me up when I begin to pout!

The bond of brotherhood is also strong.
To share a last name is a special treat.
My brother helped me out when things went wrong.
A brother is a friend you can not beat!

BUY ME CANDY AND TOYS!

It's hard to think my Grandma is Mom's Mom;
She must have been born many years ago.
With glasses on, she's strict, but also calm;
I can't believe the things that she must know.

I wonder if she made my Mom do things,
Like clean her room, the dishes and the sink.

She knows the words of old time songs she sings;
And tests my math and really makes me think.

If I designed the world, I'd make her rich;
She'd buy me candy, fancy games and toys.

The tailor, not my Grandma'd sew the stitch
That patched the pants I got from older boys!

But wait, no holiday has gone without
A lovely present from my Grandma dear.

She whispers in my ear and will not shout
When she corrects me, so my folks don't hear!

As for the candy, fancy games and such:
I get enough, but keep from getting fat.
Some rich kids have a problem with too much.
I'm happy with her and the place I'm at.

HOW MANY GRANDPAS DO I WANT?

I've got two Granddads and they're not alike;
One's quite laid back and likes to watch TV.
The other one jumps on the extra bike
And goes on picnics with a friend and me.

If I remade the world, I'd make four Gramps,
And they'd compete to think up things to do.

One Gramp would help me get and mount my stamps;
The others would prepare list or two!

34

The list would have a ton of things I treasure.
Like baseball games and films with scary stuff.

I'd spend the hours with each on some new pleasure;
Until I finally had done enough!

I guess I must admit two Gramps are good;
My plan for fun would keep me out of school.

These two give me a lot: the best they could.
To change this I would have to be a fool!

So Grandpa, if you have a bit of time,
This Saturday would be just great with me:
Stop by my house a little after nine,
And find what our Museum has to see.

MOM'S SISTERS LOOK LIKE HER!

My aunts are just like mothers, more or less;
Mom's sisters look like her and she like them.
They scold like her when I have made a mess;
But one of them is really quite a gem.

Aunt Susie always takes my point of view;
And kisses bumps and bruises when I fall.

At home she also has a kid or two;
In my new world Aunt Sue would rule us all!

The other aunts are nice enough, I guess;
I know it isn't proper to compare;

But dear Aunt Sue brings lots of happiness.
My world would have a lot of "Susies" there!

In my few years I've learned a thing or two;
Like aunts can be unique in their own way.

If variations in our friends were few;
The world would be quite boring every day!

So God made people different in their looks.
And in the way they think and talk and act.
He made the world: The stories in my books
Prove God's the best creator: THAT'S A FACT

NOTE TO PARENT/TEACHER:

My Brother's Pants Don't Fit Me is a "Midas Touch" type of "read-to" story for children up to age 90 who love the ridiculous in words (and pictures for kids who don't read). Intent is to challenge with concepts and 'big' words to be explored at the appropriate age with an adult reader at "story time." When the revised plan doesn't exactly satisfy, the child makes the real world acceptable. The writer, Dr. If (pen name used by Gordon Ralph), encourages emails to the kid-friendly author listed on the cover by writing Dr.If@remakingtheworld.com. Future books in this series, will be published by KidAndParentsPress.com. The books will be part of a "'Remaking' the World" series issued in 4 versions:

1) Black line for parent/teacher $8 (may be used as coloring book)

2) Color editions $12 (Cover is example of water color illustration)

3) Electronic downloadable black and white or color editions $8

Parents or teachers will encourage questions raised at different levels of understanding based on age. For example, kids have different features, bodies and skin colors. Talk about how the stories apply to a child's world at that age. It's a chance to address topics that don't normally arise daily. Each book has 8 stories. A couple of them for bedtime reading should be fun for old and young.

BOOKS AND RESOURCES

'REMAKING' THE WORLD SERIES: For further info and target publication dates, write: Dr.If@remakingtheworld.com, or see the blog at authorsden.com/gordonpralph.

SCHEDULED TITLES ARE:

THE NOSE ON THE BACK OF MY HEAD
(What IF? Let's not change our bodies!)

MY BROTHER'S PANTS DON'T FIT ME
(Family issues simmering with humor)

PARDON MY TURKEY
(Some silly ideas about farm animals)

HOLD THAT HUG
(Learning about respect for the "wildness" of animals)

Other possible subjects: Fantasy (Scary; Imagination);
Competition (Sports; School);
Fibs (Fish Tales; Big Lies);
Travel (Castle; Geography);
Transportation (Airplane & train; Boat & car);
Fun (Gadget; Toy);
Inspiration (Hero; History);
Laughs (Humor; Silly);
Self-Reliance (Scouting; Pioneer);
The West (Cowboys; Indians);
Romance (Love; Fairy tales).

Other resources will be listed and updated on the blog above.